My Cousin Katie
Michael Garland

THOMAS Y. CROWELL NEW YORK

My Cousin Katie

Copyright © 1989 by Michael Garland

Printed in the U.S.A. All rights reserved.

Library of Congress Cataloging-in-Publication Data

Garland, Michael.

My cousin Katie / Michael Garland.

  p.   cm.

  Summary: Katie's cousin looks forward to all the wonderful things she will do when she visits Katie on the farm.

  ISBN 0-690-04738-X : $ ISBN 0-690-04740-1 (lib. bdg.) : $

  [1. Farm life—Fiction   2. Cousins—Fiction.]   I. Title.

PZ7.G18413My 1989   88-356

[E]—dc19   CIP

                                                                AC

Typography by Al Cetta

1 2 3 4 5 6 7 8 9 10

First Edition

FOR NANA

My cousin Katie lives on a farm.

The big red barn is where the animals live.

The little white house is where Katie lives.

When the sun comes up, the rooster crows.
Katie wakes up early.

She helps her mother gather eggs for breakfast.

There are lots of animals on the farm. There are cows and goats and horses. There's a cat and a dog and a donkey named Margaret.

Katie knows all about cows.
They eat grass, make milk, and swat flies
with their tails.

The cat's name is Tiger.

Tiger's job is to catch mice.

On the farm there are fields of corn and lettuce. Katie wears a big hat when she helps to weed the lettuce patch.

The dusty, old tractor is very important.
Katie's father uses it to plow the fields,
spread seeds, and harvest the crops.
When the tractor is broken,
Katie helps her father fix it.

There is an apple orchard on the farm.
When it is time to pick the apples,
you fill basket after basket with big,
red juicy ones.

In the meadow flowers grow wild.
It's fun to gather great bunches of daisies,
lilies, and goldenrod.

Sometimes Katie and her mother have a picnic
by the pond where the cows come to drink.

When the sun goes down and the sky gets dark,
the cows come home to sleep in the barn.

Tomorrow I am going to visit the farm.

I can't wait to see all the animals, the apple trees,

the meadow, and the big pond.

But most of all, I can't wait to see

my cousin Katie.